YR 4

1L

9

ROSLEY

SCHOOL

Out of the Shadow

In memory of Mum and Dad

My grateful thanks to Eugene Nicholson
of Bradford Industrial Museum
who kindly helped me with my research.

Out of the Shadow

Margaret Nash

A & C Black • London

VICTORIAN FLASHBACKS

Soldier's Son • Garry Kilworth
A Slip in Time • Maggie Pearson
Out of the Shadow • Margaret Nash
The Voyage of the Silver Bream • Theresa Tomlinson

also available:

WORLD WAR II FLASHBACKS

The Right Moment • David Belbin
Final Victory • Herbie Brennan
Blitz Boys • Linda Newbery
Blood and Ice • Neil Tonge

First paperback edition 2002
First published 2001 in hardback by
A & C Black (Publishers) Ltd
37 Soho Square, London, W1D 3QZ

Text copyright © 2001 Margaret Nash
Cover illustration © 2001 Mike Adams

The right of Margaret Nash to be identified as author of
this work has been asserted by her in accordance
with the Copyright, Designs and Patents Act 1988.

ISBN 0-7136-6101-1

A CIP catalogue record for this book is available
from the British Library.

Printed and bound in Great Britain by
Creative Print & Design (Wales), Ebbw Vale.

Contents

Author's Note

This story is set in the 1840s when industrial towns in the north of England, such as Bradford, were dominated by tall mill chimneys, pouring smoke and soot over the town. People in the mills worked in hot, smelly, and very noisy conditions and they were poorly paid.

Up to 1833 children had worked in mills from a very early age. Money was short, and many parents would have sent them there as young as possible to earn money. In the worst mills young children were beaten to keep them awake. Men like Richard Oastler wrote letters comparing the conditions to slavery.

After 1833 things were a little better when the Althorp Act was passed, forbidding the employment of children under nine in factories, and saying older children should not work more than eight hours a day. It also said that children should have at least two hours of schooling a day.

Mill-owners particularly wanted children small enough to crawl under the spinning machines, to tie the ends of yarn which had split. They, like Will in the story, were called pieceners. The job was dangerous, as to avoid the snapping jaws of the machine the pieceners had to bend their bodies in a way that made their knees ache.

In the 1840s, men following the Chartist movement fought hard for better conditions in mills. They tried peacefully at first, but when this had no effect they began disrupting mills with violence and riots.

Thanks to awareness stirred up by Chartism, and to educated men like Richard Oastler and John Wood, who appealed constantly for better conditions, things continued to improve. In 1847 the Ten Hour Bill was passed, which limited the working day to ten hours, and many people who worked in the mills in the first half of the nineteenth century have surprisingly happy memories of those days.

The characters in the story, the names of mills, or mill-owners, are purely fictitious.

1 ☀ Trouble at School

'Quick, Will. Wake up. The bell's ringing.' Will Barraclough raised his head off the desk as his friend Alice flipped her hand across his head. Oh no! He'd fallen asleep again and missed playtime. Alice rolled her skipping rope round its handles. 'Come on, I've sneaked in early to warn you.' He stretched his arms above his head, and yawned. It was all right for her. She didn't have to go to work before school like he did. She was never tired.

The rest of the class marched in, followed by Miss Priestly. Miss Priestly always came in with her head tilted upwards. Will hid a smile. Alice said she did it to stop the snooty expression sliding off her face. Miss Priestly faced the class and demanded silence. 'Sit up straight, children. The monitor will give out the arithmetic books.'

Will thrust his shoulders back, his tiredness forgotten. He was good at sums, and could often add up figures in his head without writing them down. He looked out of the window and wished, for the hundredth time, that he could go to school all day instead of working half-time in the spinning mill, but Mam needed the money he earned.

He watched Miss Priestly's arm jerking up and down as she wrote the sums on the board. Suddenly she stopped, swept towards the front row of pupils, and tugged Mary Kelly's arm.

'Out to the front, girl. I'll not have you talking in class. No wonder you can't add two and two together.' She pointed to a chair near the easel. 'Stand up there, where I can see you.' There was silence as Mary Kelly shuffled out of the row, walked to the chair and climbed onto it. Miss Priestly's face was angry, but Mary's was expressionless. She stood there with her long, orange hair hanging loose down her back. A strip of sunlight from the arched window shone on Mary's gold wire earrings making them twinkle. Will looked at her thin arms hanging from her shabby dress, but swinging defiantly. Miss Priestly snapped, 'Stand still, girl.' Mary stood still, but as Miss Priestly turned back to the board Mary wrinkled her nose and swung her arms again.

At last Miss Priestly let Mary go back to her seat. And soon after, the bell went for home-time. Will hurried outside and across the playground. The afternoon was unusually damp and gloomy for the time of year, and though it wouldn't be dark for a few hours, the lamplighter was lighting the gas lamp beside the school wall. A crowd of boys and girls was gathering to watch the magical moment when the wick popped into flame.

'There she goes,' said the man, gently closing the glass panel on the lamp. A cheer rose up as the cosy green glow spread round the playground.

Alice nudged Will. 'Listen, there's a train.' Will shot through the crowd like a pea from a pea-shooter, stuck his boot against the wall and levered himself onto the lamppost. Alice laughed. There could be no one in the whole school keener on trains than Will. He swung out from the lamppost, waving his cap, as the boys below clamoured round the post, trying to get up after him.

'What colour's the train?'

'How many carriages has it got?'

'Three green ones,' he shouted down, 'and there's masses of smoke, masses.' He stuck his cap back on his head. 'Hey, I think some of the smoke's a FIRE.'

'Fire?'

'Yeah, it looks like one of the mills.'

'Where, for goodness sake?'

Will pointed.

'Over Wibsey way. It could be Mitchell's or

Kellett's Mill.'

'Well, I hope it's Mitchell's.' Will looked down and saw his cousin Charlie looking up at him from the front of the crowd. 'And I hope it burns down to the ground. Rotten, greedy mill-owner there.' Charlie hated all mill-owners because of what had happened to his mother, and Will knew it, but he had heard there were slave drivers at Mitchell's. He'd heard kids were beaten to keep them awake. 'A bloke in our yard got sacked from there last week,' yelled Charlie, 'and he'd done nowt wrong.'

'Aye, but it were Basher Bill, and everyone knows what he's like,' said one of the boys.

'Yes, always in fights and stuff,' said another. Will slid down the lamppost and landed beside Charlie.

'Summat needs doing about these mill-owners and their horrible overseers,' said Charlie. He pinged a stone at the lamppost which made a hollow ringing sound. 'I'm going to join in some of these meetings, and help sort things out. You should too, Will.'

'Don't be stupid, Charlie. A lot of them men are just out to make bother.'

'A lot are not,' said Alice. 'They want better working conditions, that's all.'

'There you are,' said Charlie. 'Even your girlie

friend has more idea than you, Will Barraclough.'

Will winced as some of the boys did silly whistles. Charlie flung another stone. 'You're a coward. Cousin Coward, that's you.'

'Come on, Will,' said Alice. 'Let's go. Leave him and his nonsense.'

They walked down the street together as far as Will's yard. 'I expect we'll find out if it was Mitchell's tomorrow,' said Alice. 'See you in the afternoon.' Will waved goodbye, and ran down the passageway. He wasn't a coward, just didn't like bother. He sighed, took the key from round his neck and put it in the door lock.

2 ☀ Work Pains

Will woke up. His ears were cold. He pulled the blanket over his head, and snuggled deep into the warm bed. Ginny, the Knocker-Upper, would be round, tapping on the windows soon, but she didn't knock at their windows. It cost pennies, Mam said. Instead they just listened for her footsteps on the cobbles. There they went, clack clack. Will groaned and pushed back the blankets, shivering as cold air wrapped round him. He shuffled into his trousers and took his shirt and socks downstairs with him.

'Morning, love. I've filled the sink with hot water for you.' His mother put the kettle back on the kitchen range.

'Thanks, Mam.' Will lowered his arms into the water, inch by inch, letting the circle of warmth creep up them until it reached his elbows. 'Did you hear about the mill fire yesterday, Mam? It might have been Mitchell's. Do you think it was started on purpose?'

Mam shrugged. 'Could have been,' she said. 'The boss there cut wages. He sacked the men who wouldn't work for less money, and took on men who would. And there's poor Aggie Shaw with eight kids to feed, and her husband bringing in less now.'

Will dried his arms and face, and dressed. He sat at the table and put his hands round his warm mug of tea, and raised it to his mouth. He let the warm steam rise comfortingly over his lips to his nose. 'Charlie hopes the mill burns to the ground,' he said. 'He still hates the mills.'

'Well, you can't blame him can you? Losing his mother like that.' Will supposed not. Auntie Lily had worked in the rag-sorting department, and developed a dreadful cough. She'd got weaker and weaker and died when Charlie was five. 'Folks say there'll be more trouble to come. The workers are fighting back.' She shook her head. 'But I don't know if it will do any good. It's the times we live in. And you can't alter that!' Will reached for his dish of porridge and began eating.

'It must have been nice when you were a little girl, and lived in the country, keeping pigs and hens, with your father weaving at home instead of working in a mill. Why did he move here?' His mother pursed her lips.

'People did, when the mills started. More money,

you see. Now hurry up, Will. There's the coal to do.' Will shovelled the last spoonfuls of thick porridge into his mouth then went to the coalhouse and filled the scuttle. Bringing the day's coal into the house was a job he did every morning before work.

'Bye, Mam.' He stepped out into the dark morning, and joined the lines of workers in the street. They were all heading for the mill which glowed in the dimness, like a tall, yellow lantern. No one spoke much at this time of day. There was just a murmur of voices and the clatter of the clogs on the cobblestones. Will pulled his cap down over his ears and watched his breath twirl out of his mouth, and spiral into nothingness. He saw Mary Kelly pull her grey shawl around her hunched shoulders, and thought how lucky Alice was. She would still be in bed, snug and safe, in the house next to her father's grocery store.

The big mill gate stood open, letting everyone pour through, and go their separate ways. Will clomped up the stone stairs to the spinning room, hearing the deafening din from the machines get louder and louder. When he'd begun at Brayshaw's, his head had pounded with the noise, and he'd felt sick for a week, but he'd learned to put up with it.

Mr Dyson was adjusting the pins on one of the spinning frames. He stopped and began pacing round the room as workers drifted in.

'Get a move on there, Edie. I can't see anything to smile about.' Will could. Edie, a tall, thin, jolly girl, was leaving at the end of the week, to get married. He'd be jumping with joy if it was him leaving. Mr Dyson thrust a broom at Will. 'Get the place swept, young un, and be quick about it.' Will was supposed to sweep the floor every two hours, but it wasn't always easy to find the time. Already one of the women was signalling and shouting to him to mend the broken yarn on her spinning frame. Will hurried across to the machine and carefully crawled underneath it. Then, dodging its dangerous snapping jaws above him, he tied the ends of the yarn, knowing he would be at everyone's beck and call, tying ends now, until break time.

At ten o'clock the break bell rang. Will took his snap tin off the shelf, and ran down the stairs, and into the fresh air. Late autumn sunlight dotted the stone wall, making the mill yard look almost beautiful. A big spider's web glistened in the corner of the wall. Like frosted lace it was.

'We had them as big as dinner plates in Ireland.

Aren't they lovely?' It was Mary Kelly. Will straightened up.

'Better enjoy them before we have to go back in that hellhole.' Mary sniffed.

'It's better than school.'

'It never is!' Then he remembered Mary's telling-off the day before, and all the other times. 'Beastly Priestly was horrid to you yesterday.'

'I don't care.' Mary pulled herself up to her full height. 'She don't like me because I'm Irish, but I'm not scared of her.' She looked down at the cobweb. 'I may not be good at sums but there are things I am good at.' She put her arms to her sides and began kicking her legs backwards and forwards. 'Give us a piece of your bread and dripping and I'll dance for you.' Her little gold earrings twisted and twinkled, and she carried on, not giving Will time to answer.

He watched in amazement. She was like a clockwork person. Like something out of a toyshop. Faster and faster she danced. Her cheeks turned red. Her hair worked its way out of its band. She tied it back again, still dancing. At last she stopped, and held out her hand. 'Come on, hand over.'

Will pushed his tin forward. 'Go on then.'

Mary took a chunk of bread, and bit into it. 'Ta.'

She walked back towards the doorway. The back-to-work bell sounded, and Will trudged behind her.

He stood on his toes and pushed his snap tin back on the shelf. Then, seeing Mr Dyson wasn't around, he nipped out of the door, onto the back landing, to watch the bales of wool being hoisted up from the yard on huge hooks, and the big, gentle cart horse snuffling into his nosebag. He peered through the dusty window. Five men huddled together, inside the blacksmith's forge. They were standing shoulder to shoulder in a circle, as though telling secrets. One of them punched his fist in the air. The others did the same. A disturbing chill flickered down Will's spine. He shivered, then hurried back into the spinning room.

3 ☼ The Dare

A smell of bonfires drifted through the air as Will left his house after tea. Though the dark was coming in, evening was the best part of the day – the only time when he was free to do what he liked, which was going up to the hills beyond the back streets, to watch trains. Already one was hooting in the distance. He rushed through the churchyard, and through the gap in the wall, but was only halfway up a hill when the train rattled along in the distance, and he missed seeing it.

'Hard luck, Will.' He looked up and saw Alice sitting at the top. She waved. Then he saw Mary doing cartwheels beside her. He climbed up to the top.

'What are *you* doing here?' he said to Mary. Mary stuck her tongue out at him.

'Minding my own business. I've a right to be here if I wants to be. I've done my chores. Just got to feed the donkey before I goes to bed, that's all.' She stretched onto her toes, and shot her hands in the air. 'I feels like running and running, Alice. Do you?

Let's pretend we're birds.' She spread her arms wide. 'We're eagles, see, that fly high and settle on tops of mountains.' She set off running, down the hillside. Will and Alice followed, their arms stretched wide, then up the biggest hill of all, where they all flopped down panting.

Alice was the first to get her breath and sit up. She gazed down to where the candle-lit houses clustered below. 'Don't the houses down there look small?' she said. 'They're like dolls' houses.' Mary pointed to some near the beck. 'See, that's where I lives. Down Baker Fold, number two. Which one's yours, Will?'

'Albert Yard, over there,' said Will, pointing.

'Oh yes, posh eh?'

Will said nothing. No one in their right mind could call the yard where he lived posh. Posh houses had front doors and bits of garden, not steps and smelly lavs. 'You're not far from t' mill are you?'

'No, nor school.'

'Huh, school.' Mary sniffed.

'Did you go to school in Ireland?' said Will, watching the smoke from the mill chimneys curl into the air, and hang over the houses like a black pan lid.

'Mercy me, no,' said Mary. 'I wouldn't go here neither, but Aunt makes me. Uncle don't hold with it. He'd have me selling salt with him and the donkey if he could. Anyway, what you come up here for?' Will kicked a stone and watched it bounce down the hillside.

'Just messing about.'

'He comes here to watch the trains,' said Alice. 'Oh, you know that fire we saw yesterday? It was Mitchell's, and Dad heard it was started on purpose. It burned out the sorting room, but no one was hurt.' She turned to Will. 'That rough cousin of yours swaggered into our shop, shouting out about it. Grinning all over his face, Dad said.'

'Was it owt to do with Basher Bill?'

Alice shrugged. 'Don't know.'

'We'll soon hear,' said Will. Alice nodded. 'Anyway, me and Mary's come here so she can show me how to dance.'

'She's good at it,' said Will. Mary beamed.

'You can do it too.'

But Will pulled a long face. 'Not likely. It's sissy stuff. But you've got to be able to kick like anything. I bet you can't kick fast enough, Alice.'

'Go on, kick him, Alice,' said Mary. She laughed. 'Anyway, I've gone off dancing. Now there's three of us, let's do something more exciting.' Her eyes lit up. 'I know what we can do. Race you down the hill, then I'll tell.'

They landed in a giggling heap at the bottom.

'Right,' said Mary, pulling Alice up. 'Why don't we all sneak into the Dark Lantern? See what it's like inside.' Will stared at her in disbelief. Alice shook her head.

'The pub! Are you loony? It's one of the worst pubs there is, that one. There's often fights there. I'm not going.'

'Spoilsport!' said Mary. 'I bet 'im-with-the-donkey's in there.' She gave Will a shove. 'Go on. I dare you to go and look, Will Barraclough. You see if he's in there. He's got a brown jacket, long scraggy hair, and no cap.' Will rubbed his chin. 'Oh go on with you,' said Mary. 'It's a dare. I dares you to do it!' Will began walking over to the public house.

'WILL!' yelled Alice, running after him. 'Don't! It's a terrible place.'

'A dare's a dare!' he said.

'It's not as bad as our Irish pubs,' said Mary. 'Anyway...' she paused, '...it's easier for you, being a boy, so you must bring an empty beer mug out with you to make it fair.' She put her hands on Will's back and steered him gently towards the door. Will was quiet. Mam would go mad if she knew. He'd been warned by her never even to go near alehouses. 'Horrid places,' Mam had said firmly. He tried to imagine what one would be like. Surely if he went in, just the once to find out, it wouldn't matter. And he need never go in ever again.

'All you've got to do is run in at the front and out at the back,' said Mary. He clasped the door jamb, and stuck his head round the door. 'Phew, you can hardly see for smoke.'

'Go on, get in,' said Mary brightly. She gave him a shove. He hesitated.

'Here ninny, let me go first then.' She pushed in front and was suddenly gone into the smoke and din. Will and Alice ran round to the back and waited.

Mary came out grinning. 'Easy. It's packed in there. No one will notice you. Just get behind the tables and shuffle along. Make for the pillar near the door, then run out.' Will felt his heart grow heavy as stone.

'Oh, go on!' said Mary. 'If I can go with 'im-with-the-donkey inside, then you surely can. He'd have taken a stick to me if he'd spotted me.' Alice was hanging back, saying nothing. Will swallowed hard. He knew he was a bit of a softy. Other lads at school would do it. Perhaps it wasn't as horrid as Mam made out. If he went in, he'd find out. He felt a twitch of excitement, and peeped round the door frame. Then, before he could change his mind, he slid in.

4 ☼ Pub Talk

Will hadn't known what to expect, but he wasn't prepared for the roar of jarring voices that hit him. He stared up at the low, smoky ceiling, pressed his back against the wall and began feeling his way along in the dimness. Suddenly, there was a bang. He held his breath. But it was only a spark from the glowing log fire. He was already down one side of the pub. He remembered the empty beer mug he had to take out with him. All the ones he could see were half full. He was down the long wall now. Halfway. Only the last long wall to edge down. It had been easier than expected. But suddenly things went wrong.

'Move the tables back to the walls, folks,' called a voice from the hatch. 'We're in for a bit of sport here.' Will squatted down out of sight, but at once a table came near, almost hitting his leg. He crawled underneath it, hoping to get from table to table, but men came and sat on the benches. Help! He was barricaded in! Legs scissored all round him. He was trapped! There was no way he could escape from under the table. Panic shot through him. The smoke stung his eyes. He was hot. He was thirsty. He curled up and hugged his legs to his body and prayed he wouldn't be found.

Even the slate floor felt warm. He could see nothing in the murky haze except the men's boots, some laced, some not, and one pair tied with orange twine. Men were cheering and booing. They must be betting in the centre of the room. Please don't let there be cockfighting. He knew the cruel practice went on in some places. A boot kicked his ankle, making him wince. How was he going to get out of here? Suppose there was anyone here who knew Mam. Silas from their yard drank in here. He'd really delight in telling Mam he'd seen her son under a table in the Dark Lantern.

Despite the background babble Will could hear the men at the table talking. They were talking excitedly about riots, where plugs had been pulled on boilers, stopping mill machinery working. Then suddenly Will heard the word 'Brayshaw's'. He froze.

'They cut hours there once. Does the man think we're fools? He'll not do that again, by heck. We'll see to that.' Will's cheeks went hot. Sweat was pouring off him. There was a scraping noise as the bench was pushed back and one of the men stood up and yelled for more ale.

'Don't want anyone suspecting we're here for owt but the drink,' he whispered. 'Now, everyone knows the rules. If they'll not strike, we'll stop the machines.' Will felt sick. At Brayshaw's, did they mean? But Brayshaw, though tough with his men, was known to be one of the fairer bosses. No, they'd be talking about Kellett's or Dobson's where the rooms were crammed with endless machines, so the aisles were extremely narrow, and the air stinking, even at the beginning of the day.

'The men from Dobson's are behind us,' said another. 'We've many an unhappy man there, ground down with low wages.' Who were the men sitting up above? Were any of them Brayshaw's men? He couldn't tell. The room was getting noisier. He thought he heard a cockerel squawk but someone nearby started squeezing a concertina. He couldn't even hear the men now. Will huddled uncomfortably for what seemed hours.

The men left as suddenly as they had arrived. They all went together, five of them. He must get out before more people sat down at the table and fenced him in again. There were plenty of empty glasses on the table now but Will didn't care any more. He crawled under two empty tables, then over to the pillar. No one was looking. He ran outside.

It was dark as black velvet. There was no Alice and no Mary. They'd gone. The stars were out, but no moon. Everything was silent, apart from some horses whinnying softly in their stables. He was tempted to go and talk to them, stroke their long soft noses, but it was best if he went straight home. He walked down the road, back to the dark streets that led to the smelly ginnel. He hoped he wouldn't meet any rough characters there. He ran as fast as he could, his clogs clattering and their sound hitting back from the damp dark walls. He didn't stop until he reached Albert Yard.

The fire was burning low in the grate. He cut himself a piece of bread from the loaf on the table, and spread it with jam.

'*Will!*' The door opened and Mam came in. 'Where have you been all this time?'

'Playing out. I forgot the time, Mam.'

'What, in the square?'

'Watching trains and stuff, up in the hills.'

'Will, I don't mind you going out in the dark whilst it's still early, but not till this hour. I hope you kept away from the Dark Lantern. You make sure you're not near there when it gets dark. Do you hear?' Will looked away. Since his father had died his mother was always anxious.

'Mam, I'm not a baby.'

'I know, but neither are you a man – yet. I don't want you getting into trouble.' She turned to pick up a pile of socks to mend. 'And another thing, Will, I don't want you being led on by your cousin Charlie. He's mixing with all sorts of trouble-makers at the moment, I hear.' Will turned away.

'I'm going to bed, Mam.' He went upstairs, snuffed out the candle, and was soon asleep.

5 ☼ Mary's Accident

There was no time for porridge next morning. Will was up late, and brushing his hair to make it lie flat. You could be sacked at Brayshaw's if your appearance was poor.

He arrived at the mill just as the gate was being closed by the man they called 'the Penny Hoile man'. 'Wait!' Will yelled. The man smiled and opened it again.

'Quick lad, afore that bulbous-nosed boss of yours lays into you.'

Will leapt up the stairs two at a time, and into the spinning room. He bumped into Mary who was throwing an empty bobbin into one of the big baskets in the aisle.

'Hey Will, what happened to you last night?' He nudged her to shut up, for Dyson was lurching towards him, his face red and angry. He felt a hand land heavily on his shoulder.

'You're late.'

'Only a second, sir. Sorry.' The overseer ground his hand painfully into Will's shoulder. He twisted Will's ear, till Will yelled out, and tears pricked behind his eyes. The overseer leaned over him with whisky-smelling breath.

'Tuppence off your wages,' he yelled and flung him away. Will staggered against the wall, steadied himself and kicked one of the baskets. Mr Dyson smirked. He ambled up to where Edie stood at her spinning frame, and cracked the fluff-beater strap, catching her ankle. 'That's two of you fined, isn't it, Edie? And it's not yet a quarter to seven. Women like you, Edie Wright, want your tongues cutting out. Wag, wag, wag instead of working.'

Will began sweeping the floor. So Edie had been fined too, for talking. He watched Mr Dyson go back behind the frosted-glass partition, and saw the shape of his body lean against the wall.

Hunger combed Will's stomach, but there was no escape from crawling under the dreadful machines which made his knees ache like they would split. Then, just before break time, the door opened and in came Mr Brayshaw himself, with a visitor. Mr Dyson sidled out of his office, sideways, like a crab emerging from under a stone, folded his arms, and bowed to the men. He asked if he could be of assistance. 'Would the inspector like showing round?' But Mr Brayshaw sniffed, and declined the offer, suggesting Mr Dyson get back to his work.

The mill-owner took the man round himself, pointing out how clean the room was, how happy the girls looked, and saying that no one worked a minute over the allotted hours in his mill. He stopped beside Rose. 'This capable young lady takes charge in Mr Dyson's absence, and knows the routines here well,' he said. The man asked Rose questions. Will saw her bob to the men as they left. They did not bother to speak to Mr Dyson again, though Will could see the overseer peering at the two gentlemen as they passed by. Will saw him take a small bottle from his pocket, unscrew the top and put the bottle to his lips.

The visit had helped pass the time to the break. Will remembered the two slices of parkin Mam had put in his snap tin and, the moment the bell sounded, he hurried down the room to get it. Mary reached out to him.

'Tell me what happened last night.'

'Yes, in a minute.' Will reached up to the shelf for his tin. It had got pushed to the back of the shelf. He stood on one of the buffets there, and eased the tin to the front. As he grabbed the tin there came a piercing scream. Will dropped the tin and turned. Mary lay crumpled on the floor. Crumpled and still, and with her eyes shut.

'*Mary!* Oh no!'

6 ☀ Will Takes Charge

Pandemonium broke out, then quickly simmered down. Will knelt beside Mary.

'Oh, Mary. Are you all right?' But he knew she wasn't. He didn't expect an answer. Her eyes were still closed. He daren't even touch her. Instead he looked up at the other pale faces, now circling Mary. One girl was holding Mary's head, and another mopped the blood pouring down Mary's neck.

'Got her hair stuck to the belt. Lucky she wasn't dragged up to the ceiling.'

'Ooh lummy! I bet it hurts.' said Edie. She was wringing her hands and pulling a face.

'Poor little thing. Got to her in time, thank goodness,' said Rose. She put a hand on Mary's forehead.

Mr Dyson came staggering down the aisle. 'Get her aunt. Fetch some water.'

Everyone scuttled about, trying to help. Will glanced at the belt stretching up to the pipes. Strands of Mary's orange hair were still going round with it. It was every girl's dread that they would get their hair caught in the machines. Thank goodness he was a boy. Luckily, the belt had only taken a switch of Mary's hair.

Mr Dyson stood gazing at Mary, who now lay cradled in Rose's arms, whilst Edie held a pad to her head. Mary's eyes flickered open. Will sighed with relief, but Mary's face was as white as a wax candle. The accident had happened so quickly. And those wretched machines were still pounding away. They'd not be turned off. They ruled the place – those huge long spinning beasts with giant wire teeth. How he hated them. The door at the other end of the room flung open and Mary's aunt burst in.

'Oh, mercy me!' she cried. She knelt beside her niece, and took her into her arms. 'Aren't I always telling you to tie your hair back properly? You could have been scalped.' Mary started to cry. Her aunt babbled on in her strong Irish accent. She seemed unable to stop. 'Oh Mother of God, child.' She crossed herself and stroked Mary's arm. 'Thank God you're spared, though.'

'Let me wind this bandage round her head,' said Mr Dyson, suddenly trying to act as if he was in control. He was making a clumsy attempt when Rose came through the knot of people with a mug of tea, and took over. Will eased some sacking between Mary's back and the pillar, so she could sip the tea which he now held up to her lips.

'You'll be all right, Mary,' he said. 'Drink this sweet tea.' Mary slurped the warm liquid. She stopped trembling. She was a brave girl was Mary Kelly. Braver than he, Will, would have been.

'I'll make arrangements for her to be taken home,' said Mr Dyson, and left the room. Will blew out his cheeks. It was hot and airless in the room. He rolled up his sleeves, and ran his hands through his sweaty brown hair.

Mr Dyson returned with thick, grey blankets, and Edie wrapped one round Mary.

'That'll keep you warm, love.' Mary grasped the edge of it with her fingers, and pulled it up over her face.

'A driver is waiting for you down in the yard with the horse and cart, Mrs Kelly,' said Mr Dyson. He paused. 'I'll er… I'll carry her down.' He reeled against the wall. Will stepped forward.

'I'll take Mary down,' he said. 'You might fall,' and the contempt for Dyson was there in his voice, for everyone to hear. He slid his arms under Mary's thin body, and lifted her off the floor.

Rose opened the door. 'Are you sure, Will? Can

you manage?'

He nodded. 'She's only light.'

'I'll come with you.' Rose walked beside him, carrying more blankets, and Mary's aunt, now silent, followed them down the stairs.

Will stood against the stone wall, letting its coldness strike through to his skin as the driver lifted the reins and clicked his teeth at the horse. Across the cobble-stone yard lay the long black shadow of the mill chimney. It was like a finger, pointing the way out of the dreadful place. The horse neighed, and tossed its head. Then it began to walk, and the cartwheels ground down the long shadow. Rose stepped back, and stood beside Will. He no longer felt hungry. He felt as though he might never eat another thing ever. Rose put an arm round his shoulder, and without saying anything, the pair of them went back up the stairs.

The damp mist, that always hung in the room, seemed more heavy and sour than usual. No wonder men had meetings and fought the mill owners for better conditions. Will felt sick with the heat, and the oily smell of the wool, but most of all he felt sick with the drunken uselessness of Dyson. A picture of Charlie pinging the stone angrily against the lamppost, saying 'summat needed doing' about horrible overseers, sprang into his mind. Charlie was right about that. Something did need doing. But what? How? He was glad when it was time to leave and go to school.

7 ☼ Time to Act

School did not take Will's mind off Mary's horrific accident. The other kids wanted to hear all the gory details, especially the ones who didn't have to work in the mills and went to school all day. Alice was different.

'I'm going round to see her the moment we get out of here,' she said.

'Me too.' He was thankful when the class had to stand with their hands together and say the home-time prayer.

'Amen.' There was the instant shuffling of forty pairs of feet. Miss Priestly clapped her hands and demanded quiet, and when she got it, Will was surprised to hear her say a special little prayer for Mary.

Together he and Alice set off in the chilly grey afternoon, determined to find number two, Baker Fold. As they walked down the grubby back streets, Will noticed Alice looking at her boots. 'It's not clean like where you live,' he said, 'and it will get worse.' Alice hunched her shoulders. 'I don't care. Anyhow our street's full of horse muck. You've got to watch where you walk all the time.' She nipped her nose. 'And the stink of the muck cart is worse than a hundred lavs,' she said in a clogged voice.

They found Baker Fold close to Stinker Beck, pleated away off the road, a cluster of blackened houses, almost hidden. Alice knocked boldly at the door of number two, and stood looking at the peeling paintwork. Mary's aunt came to the door.

'Bless you for coming. Mary's none too good. She's hardly spoke.' Will peered beyond Mrs Kelly, into the dim room. Mary was lying on a made up bed on the floor, next to a tiny fire that sported no flames, just the odd hint of orange under its black coal.

'I can run and get a doctor,' offered Will. Mrs Kelly shook her head.

'Me husband would say 'twas a waste of money, but come in, will you? If you two stay with Mary a second, I'll get Maisie Palmer, from Arkwright Street. She knows about these things.'

They stepped inside, ducked under the line of damp washing and stood by the bed. Mary opened her eyes, and Will noticed they were a beautiful pale amber – like her hair only paler.

'I'll not go daft like Old Ma Smoker-Pipe down Cheapside, will I?'

'Not you,' said Alice. She squeezed Mary's hand, and smiled as she felt a small return squeeze. 'I bet you won't even be in bed long. I'll come and see you tomorrow. I'll come every day shall I?' Mary nodded, and then frowned in pain. Soon she shut her eyes and drifted off to sleep again. When her aunt came back with a worried-looking Mrs Palmer, Will and Alice left.

Alice said she must go home. It was getting dark and her mother would wonder where she was. She'd to help in the shop. Will didn't feel like going home. He said goodbye then stomped through the dim streets kicking stones and calling the mill and Mr Dyson the worst names he could think of. Hideous place with a spiteful, drunken, brutal boss.

On and on he went until he found himself in the middle of the town where the streets were steep. He stopped at the bottom of Ivegate to watch a horse struggling to pull an overloaded cart of barrels uphill. The poor thing's hooves kept slipping on the cobbles, sending sparks off the ground, and the man kept shouting at it and lashing it with his whip. Will turned away. It seemed all bosses treated their workers badly.

Will trudged on, looking dismally at his feet instead of the pavement, and crashed into a lamppost. He heard a loud guffaw. It was Charlie.

'Come to read the poster, have you?' Will stood back and saw a square of paper pasted on a gas lamppost. It told men to fight for their rights, end long hours and poor wages, and go to the meeting in Top Field. 'I'll be there,' said Charlie. 'And so should you, Will... still, it be no place for lily-livered folk, though there's women go. Reckon you're up to it?' Will swallowed hard.

'I've never been...'

'Hey shurr-up!' Charlie jabbed his elbow into Will's side. 'Listen to that din. There's summat going on at the Court-House.' The two boys raced along the street, and round the corner.

A magistrate was shouting from the top step of the Court-House. 'We sympathise with you workers, but using physical violence and bringing disruption to our mills will simply paralyse trade and hold up the improvement of conditions for the working class.'

'Talk sense!' someone shouted from the crowd. Arms shot up in the air.

'We're unemployed. How can we feed our families? We've nowt to feed 'em with.'

The magistrate raised his hand. 'You can work for your money. No one's stopping you. Now get home to your wives and families.' An elbow hit Will in the eye as angry men lunged around, refusing to go. Even the presence of the police didn't matter to them. Will glanced round the raw faces. Many of them stood there without coats or caps in the cold grey damp.

'Look!' Charlie stared as the Mayor of Bradston arrived, astride his tall white horse. Will gaped, open-mouthed, as the crowd parted to let this man wearing gold chains pass through. Most of them began to move away, but a hard core of fighters slung stones at the Court-House windows shattering the glass.

'Ow!' Will touched his forehead. Blood! He ran away, holding a piece of rag to it, with Charlie at his heels.

'That's nowt,' said Charlie. 'Soon heal.' Will thought of Mary's accident. True, his injury was nowt. But Mary's, that was something different. And she'd got it working for a rotten, drunken overseer, on dangerous equipment that never slowed down.

'I'm going to that meeting, Charlie.'

'We'll go together,' said Charlie. But Will wasn't ready for that.

'I'm going on my own,' he said, 'but I'll probably see you there.'

8 ☀ In the Thick of It

On Saturday mornings they always had a late meal, a sort of breakfast and dinner combined.

'You're quiet, Will.' His mother spooned potato and boiled bacon onto Will's plate. 'Is that a cut on your face?'

'Someone kicked a stone,' he mumbled, pulling his hair forward to hide the cut on his forehead.

'You've not been fighting, have you? I don't want you getting mixed up in anything. You know what I mean, don't you?' She scraped the spoon round the bottom of the pan, gathering the last fluffs of potato. Will nodded. He knew she meant getting involved with Charlie. He watched her carefully replace the pan on the kitchen range. She didn't understand. She was so gentle, just content to work hard and care for them both. He looked at the gleaming fire irons at the hearth, the well sanded stone floor, and the curtain she'd made to stretch over the range and hide the washing line. It was a comfortable home, loved and cared for, despite its shabbiness.

'Mary had an accident yesterday.' He blurted the words out defiantly, telling his mother what had happened. 'Me and Alice went to see her after school. She looked awful.' His mother stopped eating.

'Oh, love. That's dreadful.'

'And Mr Dyson was drunk.'

'No, Will, surely not. Maybe a bit tiddly?'

'Drunk, Mam. Not able to carry Mary down the stairs to the cart. Rose and I did that.' His mother got up from the table, and took the dirty pots away. Will heard them clatter into the sink.

'I wish you were out of that place.'

'But don't you see, Mam, if wages were better, I might be, or at least I might go for fewer hours, and go to school more.' He bit his lip, wishing he'd not said that. He didn't want to hurt her. She turned to face him, her hands on her hips.

'But fighting's not the way forward, Will.'

'Then what is?'

'I don't know, but I suggest you go out for some fresh air. Go and join the kids in the square and have some fun.'

Will went out into the yard and was just in time to see the water cart passing by. He raced after it, and leapt onto the back. As it went down the street others joined him, squealing with delight.

'Gerr off!' yelled the driver.

'Oh, give us a ride, mister.' The man drove on a little, then stopped.

'You're too 'eavy for the 'orse,' he said. No one moved, until he took hold of the water hose, then they all piled off and dashed, laughing and shrieking, down the street, with the spray flipping over them.

The square was full of happy children bowling hoops, and colliding with the football lads. Will didn't notice a group of girls playing blind man's buff, and walked straight into the arms of the blindfolded girl. They all laughed as she clutched him, and he struggled. He could see Edie and her fella, walking arm in arm round the edge of the square.

'Give him a cuddle from me,' she called to the girls.

Then she waved to Will. 'Trust you to get amongst the lasses, Will Barraclough.' Will felt his cheeks go hot. He broke free and ran over to the couple.

'Here's the young whippersnapper from the mill, Jim,' Edie said. She ruffled Will's hair. 'Lovely curls he's got, see.' Will walked down the street with them, pleased to be accepted. Some of the big mill lasses could turn snooty on you, especially if they were with a man. Jim was nice. He'd been to school full-time, and learned a lot, Edie said. He was glad Edie was marrying him.

As he left them he wondered if Jim went to meetings. Did Jim agree with the workers, or was he on the bosses' side? One thing had come clear in Will's own mind though. He was going up to Top Field tomorrow, to see what happened. He'd tell no one.

The weather turned. After the damp dullness of the past week, there came a cold clear snap, with sunshine on Sunday. He went to church, and Mam, being pleased with him for that, suggested he went for a long walk. 'There'll not be many sunny days now,' she said, 'and you're cooped up in that mill and school far too long for my liking. You don't want your cough coming back this winter.'

The crowds had gathered in the long field. He could see them as he walked up Prince Street with hundreds of others. The middle of the road was taken over by horses and carts sporting flags and masts. Every lamppost it seemed, carried a placard, urging workers to stand up for themselves.

'Good to see you joining us and knowing right

from wrong, lad,' said a rough voice beside him. Will looked up to a man wearing a threadbare jacket. 'Time the bosses were made to listen to us. Working our fingers to the bone for 'em has done us no good. Did you know a mill-owner over Leeds way was ambushed and murdered?' Will shook his head.

'No, sir.'

'Aye, on his way home he was. And another had his home broken into.'

A brass band started to play somewhere in front of them.

'Good rousing stuff,' said the man. 'That's what we need.'

The crowd was getting thicker and thicker. Someone pushed through, knocking Will into another man. The road was packed now. He couldn't see further than the back of the man in front of him. He was being forced along by the crowd.

Suddenly, instead of earth under his feet there was grass. They were in the field. Banners flapped above the crowd, urging men to arm and use force to fight for their rights.

Will made his way up the far slope, in order to see more. A man climbed onto a box, and suddenly the band was playing the Chartist hymn, and people were singing. As they finished, the man on the box put a metal cone to his mouth.

'Let me tell you...' he paused. 'God made all things, but he never made a slave.'

'Hear! Hear!' Cheering erupted, arms thrust upwards. There was whistling, clapping and stamping of feet. Will could feel the ground thumping beneath his feet. It was exciting.

'How does a man know what he wants when he is starving?' The man paused. 'How does a man know what he wants when he is sinking with overwork, and sees the wealthy living off his back?'

'Aye, aye,' shouted the crowd. Will joined in.

'Aye, aye.' It was true, every word of it. He could see that now. People began pushing forward. Will found himself clinging to the man in front to stop himself being shoved down the slope.

Suddenly a large woman pushed her way onto the box near the band. She drew her shawl around her shoulders, then with one hand on her hip, she grabbed the metal cone.

'I've been sacked for attending a meeting like this,' she said. 'But by God I'm going to join you men, and fight for workers. And women,' she added. '*Yes, women.*' There were cheers, but Will heard someone behind him boo-ing.

'Get the men sorted first.'

'*Humbug!* Haven't we got a woman on the throne?' she shouted. 'Time we had the vote.' A man elbowed Will out of the way, and pushed through the crowd to the front.

'Get her off. This meeting's not about women. It's about men ground down in factories.' He made as if to rush at her, but the woman suddenly hurled a stone at him, then another and another. She was taking them out of her skirt pocket. The crowd surged forwards, but the woman wouldn't stop. Everyone on the grassy slope was moving now. Will felt himself slipping into the man in front. There was swearing and yelling. Arms waved round, objects hurled over the crowd. Below, on the level ground, some men, who were already drunk, were fighting and waving sticks. Will prayed he wouldn't be pushed into them.

A soldier on horseback ripped through the men, but not quickly enough. Someone grabbed the reins of his horse, and slowed it down. Others beat the horse with sticks. The horse, its eyes wild with terror, and body wet with sweat, turned round and round. Whether it stood on a man's foot, Will couldn't see, but someone with a pike stabbed the animal, and it fell to the ground. Will felt sick. He pushed forward. To see the poor black horse, a moment ago so proud, lying shaking on the grass was too much. He forced his way through the crowds to escape. When he got to the entrance he saw Charlie.

'Get back in there, man.' He grabbed Will's sleeve. 'Fight for our rights.' A gun shot sounded.

'What the hell's that?' said Charlie. 'Not a man is it?' Will shook his head.

'It's a horse being killed,' he said and tore away, tears welling up in his eyes and rolling down his cheeks.

9 ☀ Will's Big Decision

He managed to get rid of the tears, and blew his nose hard. How could anyone do that to a horse? He thought of the lovely horses at the mill, pulling heavy carts all day, but still gentle enough to nuzzle you and let you stroke them. He thought of the woman shouting as loud as any man, so different from his mother. He could see sense in what she said, but Mam was right about the violence. What progress could be made if men got so angry? He could still hear their noise two streets away.

Will found himself wandering out of the town towards the new railway line. He stopped on the bridge where the road lifted over the tracks and gazed down at their silver lines meeting at a point in the distance.

Suddenly a funnel of smoke rose there, and a big black engine pushed out of it. On and on it came, snorting and puffing towards him. He pressed his toes into the studded metal bridge, levered himself up, and managed to get his arms and shoulders over the top so that they anchored him. It was the most powerful thing he'd ever seen, and it was here, just beneath him, whistling, roaring, steaming like a dragon, and then, suddenly, he was enveloped in swathes of its breath. He rushed to the other side of the road, wafting the sooty-smelling stuff from his face. The train thundered on towards the new station. Flecks of coal dust clung to him, and his eyes stung, but he didn't care. Engineers like Robert Stephenson and Brunel were making pathways across the country. Soon people would be able to travel miles and miles. At least some things were getting better in life. He imagined himself travelling on a train, up and down the country, out to the seaside, and never ever getting off. The excitement of it all welled up in his mind, and he surprised himself with a sudden handstand, against the studded wall. Upside down, he thought of Mary doing her cartwheels. He let his legs thump to the floor. Poor Mary. He must go to see her.

Will was surprised to see Mary sitting in the chair by the window, darning socks, and Alice sitting on the floor beside her.

'You're up!'

Mary smiled.

'Yes, Mrs Palmer said it was the shock that made me so bad Friday. I'm a lot better now, aren't I,

Alice? Apart from my head, of course. That's real sore. Want a look?' She pulled her bandage to one side. Will drew in his breath. A festering hollow, the size of a silver sixpence, was surrounded by sore red skin.

'Ugh. You poor thing.'

Mary smiled. 'Not really. Aunt's been real kind, and Alice's mam sent me some beef broth.' She pointed to a jar of brown liquid on the table.

'Mam says it will build you up!' said Alice. 'Makes you sound like a wall doesn't it?'

Mary giggled. 'Pass it me, Alice. I'll drink it now before 'im-with-the-donkey comes home and gets it.'

'What did he say about your accident?' asked Will. Mary touched her bandage.

'Oh 'e were sorry.' She leaned forward. 'By the way, what happened to you the other evening in the pub? I woke up in the night and remembered. We waited ages for you outside, didn't we, Alice?' Will's heart sank as the memories came flooding back.

'I got trapped under the table,' he said. 'I was there blooming ages.'

'Oh, mercy me.' Mary slammed her hand across her mouth. 'Oh no! You didn't get locked in, did you?' She giggled.

'No, but...' He paused.

'What? Go on, tell us.'

'I heard men talking. It sounded as though they were planning to make trouble at Brayshaw's.' Alice turned on him sharply.

'You never told *me.*'

'No.' With all that had happened, it had got pushed to the back of his mind. Mary slurped some of the broth and wiped her mouth with her hand.

'Oh, Will! You can't have done. Are you sure it was Brayshaw's? Tell me what they said, word for word.' Will tried, but couldn't remember everything. Mary leaned back in her chair.

'There's lots of trouble around, 'im-with-the-donkey says. He hears of it whilst he's on the streets. But if the mill is closed down it will be terrible, awful. We'll lose our jobs. Me and Aunt won't have enough to eat again. That's why the three of us came over from Ireland. We couldn't afford to buy food there. People were even killing their pets for food. You've got to tell someone what you heard, Will. You must.'

'Pets! How could...?'

'Yes... well some did folks said they did. Aunt and me have got work now. But if the men strike, what will we do? Everyone who can't work goes hungry these days.'

'I can't tell Mam,' said Will. 'She'd be furious with me if she knew I'd been in the Dark Lantern.'

'Then tell Mr Dyson.'

'No fear. He's no good to anyone. He was drunk when you had your accident. Did you know that?' Mary flung her darning on the ground. She put her hand to her head and frowned.

'Oh, this wretched head. If I was better I'd do something. Sure I would.' Will took a deep breath.

'I've done something.' He put his shoulders back and stood tall. 'I've been to that meeting up on the green today.'

'What!' Alice and Mary stared at him. He nodded, feeling strangely proud, even though he'd not enjoyed it.

'What you been there for? What good will that do us?' Mary was really angry now. He'd never seen her face so stern. 'They just want to spoil it for folks like us.'

'You were brave,' said Alice. 'I'd never dare go near, not on my own, but I'll go with you if there's another. What was it like?'

'*Alice*!' shouted Mary. 'Don't be daft. You're on my side. Besides women don't go to those things.'

'Some do,' said Will. 'There was one woman there, who stood on the box and shouted for votes for women.' Alice cheered. Mary screwed up her face.

'It's Brayshaw's I care about, not some ranting woman. You must tell someone, Will.'

'No Mary, I can't.'

Mary stamped her feet, then winced as the wound in her head throbbed. 'Well I know what I'd do,' she said. Her voice was getting higher and higher. There was a break in it, and a tear slid slowly out of the corner of her eye. She sniffed, and touched her head. 'I'd tell Mr Dyson, I would. I'd risk it, for everybody's sake. Getting into bother is nothing compared with being hungry and having no money.'

'I'm going home,' said Will. He went out of the door.

His mind was in turmoil. Maybe men were right to fight bad, greedy bosses. But Mr Brayshaw was supposed to be a reasonable boss. It was Dyson who was so horrible. He looked back at Mary's house as he turned out of Baker Fold. Poor Mary. And poor Mary's aunt. They were honest folk, not afraid of hard work. Suddenly he turned and ran back. He burst in through the door.

'I will do it!' he said. 'I'll tell Dyson.' Mary wiped away her tears and then she clapped her hands.

'Oh thanks, Will. It will be all right, you'll see.' She picked up her darning, and put it on her knee, but it slipped back off to the floor. 'I feel sleepy,' she said, and lay her head against the cushion.

Alice and Will left quietly.

'Why don't you come and help me weigh out pounds of sugar, and cut soap into blocks in the shop?' suggested Alice. 'I've promised my dad I would. But it's boring on my own. Sometimes I wish I worked in the mill with the rest of you.'

'You wouldn't,' said Will, 'especially if Dyson was your boss.'

10 ✿ A Guilty Secret

Will made sure he was at work early next morning. He stopped at the top of the spinning room steps, and read the notice plastered there – RULES. The letters were black and heavy, all eleven rules a dismal warning as you entered the room. You could be fined for going to the lavatory without asking, however desperate you were. Dyson quoted the rules all the time, except the one on drinking. Will pushed open the door. It annoyed him to have to tell the man what he'd heard. Dyson would get all the credit for warning the mill-owner.

He nearly fell over his boss, whose legs were sticking out from under a machine. Mr Dyson stuck his head out from the side of the machine.

'Clumsy oaf.' He turned to Rose. 'Ruddy belt's not working.' He wriggled his fat body from under the spinning frame. 'The engineer can see to it. It's his job.' He dusted himself down and walked out of the room, leaving Will gazing at the ugly grey machine. Blow! There'd be no talking to the man until the wretched thing was up and running, making money.

The engineer was with Mr Dyson until after the break, but as soon as Will saw Mr Dyson in the office on his own he went and knocked at the partition. Mr Dyson strode out dressed up really smart, and pushed him aside. Then placing his top hat on his head, he hurried to the door. Will ran after him.

'Mr Dyson...'

'Not now,' he growled. Will followed him to the top of the steps.

'But Mr Dyson. I must tell you...'

'Keep it,' he called back. He was already halfway down the steps. He'd gone! That was that! Now Will couldn't tell him, and suddenly, it was the thing he wanted to do most in the world. He should have been bolder, grabbed the man's arm. But Dyson would only have flung him aside.

'Hurray! He's gone,' said Edie, who had made straight for the window.

'Yippee!' The girls' faces broke into smiles.

'Tea, Bobbin Boy!' someone yelled, and Tom, the littlest boy there, grinning all over his face, did a silly sideways step to the back of the room to mash some.

Will tried to think what to do. He could write a note and leave it in the office for Mr Dyson to find later.

'Penny for your thoughts, Will,' said Rose. 'Which girl is it this time?'

'I bet it's young Sophie from the next room, with the blonde plait,' said Edie. 'She's always gawping at him with those big blue eyes of hers.'

'Oooh, oooh, Will.' The teasing swam round the room. He was used to their taunts, but it still made him cringe.

'I bet it's buxom Bess from next door,' said another. There were hoots of laughter.

'He'll not get his arms around her.'

'Let's start trimming up for Edie's send-off on Friday,' said the girl at the end spinning frame. She ran to the box with the Union Jack on the lid, and took out some brightly-coloured bunting.

'No,' said Rose, firmly. 'Dyson will go nutty.'

'Oh come on, blow Dyson,' said Edie, 'let's kick our heels.' She pushed Tom's bobbin skep, and sent it careering towards the wall. 'Come on.' Before you could say 'dance', the girls were in the aisle, linking arms and singing. They were kicking their legs, lifting their skirts. '*Bobby Shaftoe's gone to sea, silver buckles on his knee. He'll come back and...'*

Will escaped to the office to write his note. On the table lay a leather-bound ledger, open at the fines page. Whenever Will saw columns of figures he couldn't help adding them up. He didn't know why. It was something he did automatically. He cast his eyes down the short columns. There was only one entry for last week, and that was from Tom, who'd accidentally broken a bobbin, but the fines he and Edie had been charged a few days earlier were not there. He flicked back through the marbled pages of looped writing. Where was the one Mary had got for swearing two weeks ago? Mary had paid up, when she'd been paid. Where was Ruth's? Missing – all of them, yet Dyson fined all the time. Will bet Dyson was keeping the money for himself. He beckoned Rose across to the office.

'What you doing in there, you loony? You'll get me sacked if Dyson finds out.'

'Come and look here.' He stabbed the open page. Rose peered at the figures.

'But where are all the fines?'

'Missing,' said Will, 'and see, last year there's only about twenty, yet he fines someone every week.' Rose pulled the big book towards her.

'The cheat, the lying cheat. He's keeping the money. And it looks good for him if there are no fines, Brayshaw thinks he's managing us well, and we're too hard-working to be fined.'

Suddenly there was a cluster of women round the office.

'What's up?' said Edie. Rose kept her arm on her friend, but told the others to get back to work.

'Flipping 'eck!' said Edie. 'He's fiddling the books. He's not entering the fine money we've paid him.'

'Will spotted it,' said Rose.

'But what can we do about it?' said Will. He rubbed his sweaty palms down his trousers. Rose bit her lip.

'We can't tell him. He'd go mental. He'd sack us. I can just see his face puffing, and his strawberry nose turning purple.' They laughed then went quiet. Suddenly Edie threw her arms in the air. 'I've got it. Leave it with me.'

'What?' said Rose.

'You'll see!' Edie gave a whoop of joy and danced back down to the other end of the room, to where the girls were either eating their sandwiches by the window, or trying to sleep in the corner.

No amount of pleading would persuade Edie to

tell Rose and Will what she planned. In the end Will's hunger got too much and he left Rose promising Edie fruit buns galore, if she'd tell. But Edie was shaking her head and Will knew she wouldn't tell. He hoped whatever it was worked though.

11 ☀ Eavesdropping

Will fingered the two pennies Mam had given him, and wandered off towards the pie shop down Main Street. The warm meaty smell drifting towards him suddenly made him hurry. Old Ma Briggs's mutton pies were the best in town.

He walked down the street, sinking his teeth into the pie and enjoying the delicious taste of the meat and juices which smothered his mouth. At the corner he stopped to wipe the gravy from his chin, and lick his sticky fingers.

A group of men stood further down the street, by the gas lamp, their heads nearly touching. Will froze. They were the men he'd seen in the forge at Brayshaw's. Except now, 'Basher Bill' was with them. There was no mistaking him with his black hair. He stood half a foot higher than the others. Had they been the five men in the Dark Lantern? One was looking at him. Will walked uneasily past them.

'If they can do it we can,' one of them said.

'With pikes,' added another. Will felt sick. Pikes

– those long, pointed staffs? He wanted to run away, pretend he'd not heard them. But he mustn't, not now. He must try and hear more. He leaned against the wall and shook his foot, pretending there was a stone in his boot, then limped into the cake shop doorway. He sat down on the cold, hollowed step, and slowly undid his boot lace, straining to hear the men.

'Right, then we're all set for Brayshaw's, Tuesday. He's always there Tuesdays. We'll show him. We'll stop his men being so keen to work.' Will's hands trembled as he eased the boot off his foot. He shook the boot hard, and looked inside. They'd stopped talking now. Out of the corner of his eye he could see them. They were all watching him.

'Hey *kid!* Yes, you. How many stones have you got in that there boot of yours?' Will didn't answer. He put his foot back in the boot, and quickly tied the lace. Glancing along the ground, he caught sight of the man's ugly boots. They were big, black toe-capped ones, capable of giving a hearty kick. He gasped. They were tied with orange twine! They were the boots from under the table in the Dark Lantern!

'I know you,' said another man. Will recognised

him as the blacksmith from Brayshaw's. The man rolled his newspaper and lunged towards him. 'You're one of Brayshaw's half-time kids.' He raised the newspaper at him. 'Clear off before I clout you one, you nosy little beggar.' Will scrambled to his feet. He sped round the corner. His heart was drumming fast. He didn't go home. He ran straight to school, through the gates and bumped into Alice. 'Alice, oh Alice!'

She steadied him. 'What's up?'

He slumped to the ground, breathless. 'I've just heard some men. They're planning to attack Brayshaw's.'

'Don't be daft.'

'They are. They are. I tried to tell Dyson earlier, but he wouldn't listen, and now he's gone to the wool exchange.' He could hear his voice getting more and more desperate. 'It will be ages before he's back – it might not be till tomorrow.'

'Steady on, Will.' But Will wouldn't be steadied. He thought of his promise to Mary, and of his mum needing his money. A promise was a promise. He told her about the men he'd seen in Brayshaw's yard, as well. Her eyes widened. 'Well, you can tell him tomorrow.'

'No,' said Will. 'It will be too late.' The school

bell rang. Miss Priestly had come into the yard. Will stood up. 'Those men said Tuesday for Brayshaw's. It's Monday today! What can I do?'

'Go and tell Mr Brayshaw yourself, that's what,' said Alice. Will swallowed hard. 'What, on my own?'

She nodded. 'Now. You have to.' In his mind Will could see the big, posh mill house hiding away at the end of the lane, behind high walls. He couldn't.

Children were running across the playground from all corners to line up in front of Miss Priestly, and Miss Priestly was watching them. Will took a deep breath. Then, before he could change his mind, he ran out of the school gate. He flattened himself against the wall. There was a skidding sound. He turned his head sideways. Alice was there beside him.

12 ☼ The Warning

Will looked at her gratefully. 'Come on, run for it.' They charged down the road, not slowing down until they were past the workers' houses, and into the lane. 'What shall we say when we get there?'

'Tell him what you know,' said Alice.

'Even the pub bit?'

Alice hesitated. 'Well that's not as important now as the men in the street, is it?'

He pointed to the double iron gates at the beginning of the sweeping drive. They were padlocked.

'We'll climb over.'

Alice fingered the prickly hedge with her fingertips. 'They're high, Will!'

'I'll give you a hitch up.'

'I'm not going over first.'

But when they got there, Alice found she had to, if Will was to help her. He bent down and told her to step onto his shoulder. 'Grab the railings and quickly heave yourself up. I can't stand your weight for long.'

'We're trespassing you know,' she said, as she jumped down from the gate. 'What if they shoot us?'

He laughed, suddenly feeling bolder, and followed her.

'Or we get caught in a mantrap?'

'Or hung drawn and quartered!'

'Or set on by dogs.'

She pushed him. 'Shut up, you daft ha'porth.'

Will looked across the green lawns. Everything was clean and neat. Fresh autumn leaves were wafting over the grass, and a few late roses still peeped over the hedge near the house. Lucky rich man. Will thought of the black mill building standing on cobblestones, slippy with dirt. He thought of the greying white walls in the spinning room, streaked with ugly rust marks near the pipes. Why was he trying to save the mill anyway? If it closed he wouldn't have to get up in the dark mornings to go there. He wouldn't have aching knees, all morning, from grovelling under the spinning frames. But he knew why. Most of the people he knew and liked worked in mills. Without the mills what would they do for money?

They were at the big fancy door with its stained-glass panels and brass letter box. Alice looked at him, then took a deep breath and rapped the shiny knocker. Will stood with his hands behind his back. Would Mr Brayshaw even bother to see them? His heart beat as if trying to get out of his chest. Someone was coming down the hall. A maid, dressed in black and white, opened the door. Will took off his cap.

'Please could we see Mr Brayshaw?'

'He's busy,' she snapped. 'Wait there.' A lady in a long, blue, rustling dress swept forward. She asked them in and shut the door behind them.

'What is it, children?'

'We've something important to tell Mr Brayshaw, ma'am,' said Alice, giving a little bob. Will looked at her with admiration. She always knew what to say. And she sounded so grown up. He explained quickly about having heard some disturbing talk in the street. The lady hesitated a moment, before replying.

'Go into the lounge and I'll tell my husband.' They stepped into a large, square room with big windows. Will had never seen such a light room, nor furniture which shone so you could see your reflection in it. There were rugs on the floor, big heavy ones that nearly reached the edge of the room, and shelves of books.

'Do sit on the couch,' said Mrs Brayshaw. 'My husband won't be long.'

She sat in one of the big leather chairs, and asked them about themselves. Alice told her about her father's shop, and Will said how he liked school and wished he could go full-time.

'And he's wonderful at sums,' added Alice.

'All children should have some schooling,' said Mrs Brayshaw. 'At least you've got that.' As she spoke, Will heard footsteps in the tiled hallway.

Mr Brayshaw appeared in the doorway. He had a moustache that stretched the width of his broad face. He did not look pleased.

'Your two visitors,' said his wife extending her arm out towards them. 'Alice and Will.'

Mr Brayshaw folded a piece of paper, and tucked it neatly into his top waistcoat pocket. He laced his fingers across his large stomach. 'And what brings you here, children?'

Will explained how he'd come across the men on the street corner, and overheard what they'd said. Mr Brayshaw looked grim.

'As if I hadn't enough problems.' He stomped across to the window. 'Mitchell's men are behind this, I bet. Were any of those men Brayshaw's men do you know?' Will looked down at his feet. 'Come on, out with it, lad.'

'There was one, sir… the blacksmith, sir.'

'The blacksmith! Is there no loyalty in my mill?' Brayshaw put his thumbs in his waistcoat pockets, and twitched his lips. He began pacing the room.

'Lots of us are loyal,' cried Will. 'Sir.'

The big man raised himself onto his toes. He had a sour expression on his face. 'Tell me lad, does Mr Dyson know about this?

'N… no sir. I tried to tell him, honestly sir, but he, he…'

'He wouldn't listen,' finished Alice. 'He walked away.'

'He had to go out, sir.'

'Oh, indeed,' said Mr Brayshaw. His shoulders dropped and some of the anger seemed to disappear. 'Well, never mind. I shall be speaking to him very soon about certain matters. You did the right thing coming to tell me, in that case. And mark my words, we'll be ready for the trouble-makers if they dare set foot inside our gates, if they dare even march up the road. There's no man going to spoil what I've made. And there's none going to put my loyal workers out of a job.' He slapped his hands on their shoulders. 'They'll not find it easy getting into Brayshaw's. Come on now, I'll take you back to the main road.'

Will felt like a prince, being taken down the curving drive by two dapple-grey horses. Alice was speechless with the wonder of it. Mr Brayshaw shook their hands when they'd got down from the carriage. 'You can be proud of yourselves,' he said. 'Thank you.'

'I'm glad we went,' said Will, as they reached the end of his ginnel.

'Me too,' said Alice. 'And he said we should be proud of ourselves.' She laughed. 'Do you feel proud, Will? I think I do.'

He tipped his head to one side.

'Yes, I reckon I do, for Mary's sake.'

13 ☀ Attack

'Mary!' Mary was waiting at the mill gate next morning. She still had the bandage round her head. 'Are you all right?'

'Sure – at least for the morning, I reckons. I couldn't wait to hear what Dyson said. You did tell him didn't you?'

'No.'

'WHAT! Oh Will, you promised. You pig.' She pushed him hard, so he reeled against the wall. He laughed. 'You coward. You...'

'Shurr-up and listen, Mary. Me and Alice went to Mr Brayshaw's house. We told him instead.'

'You nivver! I don't believe you.'

'I did, so there,' he explained as they climbed the stairs. He told her about seeing Basher Bill and the other men in the street.

Mr Dyson was standing at the top of the stairs. His mouth dropped open as he saw Mary.

'Glad you're back,' he said, flatly. Mary walked past him with her nose in the air. Dyson gripped Will's wrist, twisting it as he did so. 'Not so fast, my lad. What's this about you visiting the boss? I'm the one you should have told.' He prodded his chest. 'Me.'

'I tried to,' said Will. 'Remember?'

'Well I hope you knew what you were doing. Now get a move on. We've been here all night checking the place is secure.' He cracked the strap in front of Will, who didn't move. 'You heard me.' He cuffed Will round the ears, making them sting, then walked away. For the first time ever, Will didn't jump to it, but slowly picked up the broom.

'The mob won't stand a chance if they come,' whispered Rose.

'Why are you whispering?' asked Will.

'No one else knows.'

Will looked round. Everyone was working silently as usual. Mr Dyson was dealing with a delivery of yarn. 'But what if nothing happens?' said Will.

'I'll be glad,' said Rose. Will was beginning to wonder if he would be. Dyson would gloat. He might even tell Mr Brayshaw that the boy Barraclough lied, and wasn't to be trusted. What then? He'd be sacked! What would Mam do? These thoughts gnawed away at him as he grovelled under the machines.

The break bell cut off his thoughts like a knife. Mary pounced on him. 'I want to know everything. What were the curtains like, Will?'

'Long and red and tied back with sashes.'

'Were they velvet? Tell me more.' She was like a limpet, clinging to him.

'There was a vase of pink flowers on the table, and a lamp beside one of the armchairs, mirrors on the wall, and patterned wallpaper.'

Mary suddenly let go of his arm. 'I can hear voices! And it's not folks in the back streets. Listen, it's getting louder.' Will tilted his head. She was right. He felt his legs weaken, his stomach clamp. He felt he was in the middle of a dream. But workers were hurtling past him now, rushing down to the gate.

'It's the mob.' 'It's the mob!' came the cries. 'Get back inside, everyone. Back.' The men were returning, falling over themselves to get inside the building.

'Mercy me!' Mary grabbed Will's hand and the two of them raced up the stairs. They stood on the landing watching Mr Dyson lock and bar the door below. His voice came up the stairs, telling them to get in the spinning room and stay there, and then he was gone. But Will wasn't going in. He pressed his face against the cold glass window. The mob were hurling themselves against the gate like wild beasts. They were scrambling over. They were in the yard. 'Mary, they're here.' Up the yard they came in droves, some with sticks, then stopped.

'Come and join us, Brayshaw's workers! Stand up for your rights!'

'Holy Mother!' Mary knelt on the stone window sill, and crossed herself.

'A fair day's wage, for a fair day's work,' chanted the men. A huge man with shoulders as broad as doorsteps pushed forward. It was Orange Laces. 'Brayshaw, Brayshaw, we want Brayshaw!' More girls pushed behind Will.

'Look, there he is,' said Edie. Will could hardly breathe for the weight of the girls piling up behind him. Everyone saw the boss walk out alone, towards the men. Someone threw a stone. He held up his hand to them.

'This is a fair and well-run mill.' A sneering cry went up from the men.

'You've cut the hours in this mill. Call that fair?' Will looked at the men. They were a poor, scrappy lot, many in ragged clothing. 'We come to say what we have to say, peaceably. We want full work and wages back in this mill.'

'When the work comes in there will be.'

Basher thrust his arm in the air. 'Well, folks should go on strike till then.' He turned to the few workers who were lined up against the wall. 'Are you listening men? Strike! Strike!'

Will spotted Charlie in the crowd, standing beside his father, and the pair of them were shouting fit to burst their lungs.

'Strike! Strike!'

'If they do, I'll have to get men who will work,' said Mr Brayshaw. A clog came whirling from the mob.

'We'll stop your mill. We'll pull the plugs from the boilers.'

'You'll have to pull this mill down before it will stop,' yelled Mr Brayshaw. The window glass was steaming up from Will's breath. He rubbed a space. Mr Dyson was out there now.

'The militia is on its way,' he called out. The men jeered. A pikestaff flew at the mill door. Stones followed it, thudding against the solid oak.

'Oh, what if they get in here?' said one of the girls, clawing at her skirt. The girl beside her started crying.

'They won't,' said Mary.

Suddenly up the yard the militia swept, blue-jacketed figures on proud horses, waving muskets and cudgels.

'They're surrounding the mob,' Will said. He used his elbows to try and force the girls off his back, for more and more wanted to see what was happening.

'Go, the lot of you,' ordered the militia captain, 'Before you're thrown into York Castle.' The horses ploughed their way through the mob and the men could only dive between their legs and rush for the gate.

Within seconds they'd gone, leaving an empty yard apart from odd stones and an old clog, and a few stragglers. It was over.

'That did it,' said Mary.

'Yes,' said Will, flatly. He was watching the last of the bent and shabbily-dressed men lumber to the gate. He sighed. He suddenly noticed the silence. Everything was quiet, too quiet. Only then did he realise the spinning machines had, for once, been turned off. He went through the doorway and joined the others.

The women were bunched together in the aisles. Some were crying.

'Cheer up,' said Edie. 'I'm going to make us all some tea.'

She was passing the mugs round when Mr Brayshaw came in. He looked tired, but not ground down like some of the men in the yard, Will noticed. Mr Brayshaw apologised for the disruption, saying times were hard for both the mill-owners and the workers. He assured them trouble-makers would be sacked. 'I want fairness in this mill,' he said firmly. He turned to go. 'The machines will be turned on, but those who wish to may go home.'

They heard his footsteps going down the stairs.

'Phew!' said Edie. She flopped onto the bench beside the pipes. 'Anyone seen Dyson?' No one had.

'A pity the mob didn't get him.'

'I'm off,' said Will. 'I must tell Alice. Coming, Mary?' Mary pulled her shawl from its wall hook.

'Sure I am.' She touched her bandage. 'I'm still an invalid you know.'

14 ☀ Out of the Shadow

Saturday dinner-time, when the mill closed, was the time Mr Brayshaw chose to thank his loyal workers, by offering them a drink in the yard. Alice had come along too. Will was pouring lemonade from one of the jugs on the trestle table when Mary sneaked up behind them, and put her hands over Will's eyes.

'Guess who?' she said. She took her hands away and Will turned round. Mary posed. 'Do you recognise me in my new bonnet?'

'Where did you get it?' asked Will, laughing. 'You look like Beastly Priestly with that snooty look on your face.'

''Im-with-the-donkey,' said Mary. 'A rich lady gave it him for two blocks of salt.'

'The rose on the side is a bit battered,' said Alice.

Mary touched the faded rose. 'That don't matter.'

Edie came running over. 'Had to come,' she said, 'just to see what Brayshaw says.'

'But you're getting wed, aren't you?' asked Will.

'That's three hours away. You're all coming to watch, I hope. There's loads of grub. Where's Rose?'

She ran off again.

'Can't see Dyson,' said Mary.

'Huh! Not like him to miss a drink,' said Will.

A hammer banged on one of the tables, and Mr Brayshaw's voice rose above the chatter. He coughed.

'I'll not keep you, this chilly morning. I've not a lot to say, except how regrettable the riot was last Tuesday, and to thank those of you who stayed loyal to Brayshaw's.' He put his hand to his mouth and gave another important little cough. 'This mill spins some of the best worsted material in the world, and you can be proud of yourselves for that.' He raised his tankard. 'Here's to rising orders, which will come, and to a rise in hours and money for everyone.' Glasses were raised and many of the people cheered, but not everyone, Will noted. He saw one man without a drink spit and walk away.

'One more announcement,' said Mr Brayshaw. He was raising himself on his toes, as Will had seen him do in the big house.

'The trouble-makers have been sacked, and for those of you in the spinning room, Mr Dyson will no longer be your overseer. A new man will begin next week.'

'Hey, wonderful!' said Will. Mary jumped up

and down, clasping her hat to her head.

As he strode away, Mr Brayshaw took his silk handkerchief out of his pocket, and mopped his brow. A piece of paper came out with it and fluttered to the ground. Alice darted forwards and picked it up.

'It's a page of an account book,' she said. Will grabbed the paper from her. It was the fines page out of the spinning room ledger, the one with only half the fines in.

'How did he get that?'

Edie was at his side. She picked it from Will's fingers.

'I tore it out, as soon as you'd gone, and sent it to Brayshaw's home. He can't do owt to me. I've left.'

'But what could he tell from that?' said Mary. 'He won't know about the ones that weren't there would he? He wouldn't know we'd paid 'em.'

'He would,' said Edie. Her eyes shone. 'My Jim wrote me a note to Mr Brayshaw, see, explaining about the missing fines, and that went to his house with the accounts page. It's thanks to Jim he's gone.' She smiled. 'He mentioned the drink too. He said... wait a minute... I've a copy here.' She drew a bit of paper from her pocket, '*Whilst it may not be my b...* You read it Will. You're better at it than me.'

Whilst it may not be my business, Mr Brayshaw, I have to say I am dismayed to hear that your overseer partakes of the bottle when on duty.

In view of the dangers of accidents with machinery I feel it must be against all the rules.

Yours faithfully,

James Boothroyd.

'Look, Brayshaw's coming over to us,' said Alice. 'And there's your mother with him, Will.'

'What, my mam? Never!' But he could see her in her grey coat.

Mr Brayshaw held out his hand. He was smiling. He shook Will's hand, and Alice's, and Mary's.

'It's thanks to you three we were prepared for the mob,' he said.

Mary bobbed neatly. 'Me, sir?'

'Yes. You were involved I hear, despite your nasty accident. You're a brave girl, Mary.'

'Thank you, sir.' Mary bobbed again. He turned to Alice, and gave her a parcel.

'This is for you, Alice.'

'Oh thank you, sir.' Alice unwrapped it. Inside was a book with pictures and maps.

'It's about people in other countries, and the foods they produce. You'll be able to see where some of the food in your shop comes from.'

He turned to Will. 'You like school Will, I believe. Good at figures, I understand. I've had a word with your mother here, and both of us think you should go to school full-time.'

'But, sir...'

'I'm prepared to pay for you to go full-time until you are fourteen. After that you should get a chance to further your education.'

Will glanced quickly at his mother. How would she manage without his money? He didn't earn much but it was more than his school fees of twopence a day. Mr Brayshaw seemed to read his thoughts.

'I've had a word with your mother, lad. I'm prepared to pay you your usual wage as well. You start Monday.'

Will could see his mother smiling.

'But... sir... thank you.' He couldn't think what else to say. Thank you wasn't enough. His head was swimming with the wonder of it all.

'And now, Mary,' said Mr Brayshaw. 'You don't like school, eh?'

'No, sir.'

'What will you do when you leave then?'

'Work in your mill I expect, sir.'

'You may indeed.'

Will suddenly remembered the socks Mary had mended. 'You could work in a burling and mending department, Mary.'

'You could,' said Mr Brayshaw. 'There will be double money in your pay packet next week, lass. Treat yourself.'

'Double money, Will!' squealed Mary. 'Imagine!' But Will's mind was too full of school to think of anything else. He'd get an education. He'd be like Jim. Be able to write letters, understand the world better, understand people, and maybe, just maybe, he'd be one of the many men striving to get better conditions for people like Mary. Suddenly Mary started dancing.

'Alice, I never did teach you to dance, did I?' Up and down she bobbed, kicking her legs faster and faster. The blue ribbons from her bonnet streamed out behind her. Everybody turned to watch. When she finally stopped they all clapped. Mary's face shone with happiness, and she finished off with a curtsey.

'And now,' said Rose, 'Off to Edie's wedding, eh?' She grabbed Mary's hand, and Alice's. 'Come on, girls.'

Will took a last look at the mill. There it stood, rearing above them with its tall chimney. And on the ground lay its long shadow, still pointing the way out. He ran down to the end of the shadow. Then he plunged his hands to the ground and did a cartwheel into the sunshine.

Glossary

Ginnel
(Northern English) an alleyway or narrow passage between buildings

Penny Hoile man
Hoile means hole. In this context it means the space left by an open door ('put wood in't 'oile' meaning 'close the door'!) The Penny Hoile man sat at the entrance of the mill and noted the workers who arrived late. They were docked a penny from their wages.

Piecener
Children who worked in the mill joining the ends of yarn together under the machines (like Will in the story)

Skep
A wooden or wicker basket